To my husband, Michael.
Thank you for loving everything that
is different about me.

WWW.MASCOTBOOKS.COM

Paws and Think!™: We Are All Different

For more information, please contact:
Mascot Books
560 Herndon Parkway #120
Herndon, VA 20170
info@mascotbooks.com

CPSIA Code: PBANG0717A
Library of Congress Control Number: 2017905828
ISBN-13: 978-1-68401-266-4

Printed in the United States

PAWS and THINK!™

WE ARE ALL DIFFERENT

MIRANDA MITTLEMAN

ILLUSTRATED BY INDOS STUDIOS

My fur is so neat,
just look at me!

I'm black and white
with spots on my paws and belly!

My favorite thing to do
is go to the park.

I like to meet my friends
and give a hello bark!

But why do I look
so different from the others?

No one else has my spots
or my colors.

Other dogs are all brown
or solid jet black.

Some are snowy white
with no spots on their backs.

And some dogs are a simple,
shiny slate gray

With nice, sleek coats
that gleam all day.

But they all play with me
and they don't seem to care

About all of my spots
or the color of my hair.

One day I saw a dog
sitting alone by a tree.

He was short and wrinkly
and had more spots than me!

So I barked, "Ruff! Ruff! Hello!"
and I played with him too.

I welcomed him proudly
to our doggie crew!

Each day after that
I'd find a new friend,

And before I knew it,
our colors would all blend!

We may not all look the same but that's okay.

We can still get along and we can still play!

So the next time you meet someone
different from you,

PAWS and THINK!
You are different too!

Miranda Mittleman grew up in Baltimore, Maryland, where she earned her bachelor's degree in marketing from Towson University. She's an avid runner, has a black belt in karate, and was even a contestant on *Wheel of Fortune!* But her true passion has always been poetry. She can recite most poems from her childhood by heart and was inspired to write the ***PAWS and THINK!***™ series while living in the city with her husband, Michael, and their playful mutt, Weaver.

Have a book idea?
Contact us at:

560 Herndon Parkway
Suite 120
Herndon, VA 20170
info@mascotbooks.com | www.mascotbooks.com

See what lesson I dig up next!